W9-BUM-906

PATTY'S PUMPKIN PATCH

WRITTEN AND ILLUSTRATED BY

TERI SLOAT

G. P. PUTNAM'S SONS • NEW YORK

To my cousin Patty – T. S.

The artwork was prepared with acrylic on 300wt. Arches cold press watercolor paper, with oil pastel overlay. Pastel grounds were spread over the acrylic and oil pastel to allow for final detailing with acrylic.

Copyright © 1999 by Teri Sloat.   All rights reserved.
This book, or parts thereof, may not be reproduced in any form without permission in writing from the publisher. G. P. Putnam's Sons, a division of Penguin Putnam Books for Young Readers, 345 Hudson Street, New York, NY 10014.

G. P. Putnam's Sons, Reg. U.S. Pat. & Tm. Off. Published simultaneously in Canada.
Printed in Hong Kong by South China Printing Co. (1988) Ltd.
Designed by Gunta Alexander. Text set in Icone.
Library of Congress Cataloging-in-Publication Data
Patty's pumpkin patch / Teri Sloat. p. cm. Summary: Rhyming text and illustrations featuring the letters from A to Z follow Patty as she plants pumpkins and watches them grow. [1. Pumpkin—Fiction. 2. Alphabet. 3. Stories in rhyme.] I. Title.
PZ8.3.S63245Pat 1999 [E]—dc21 98-17475 CIP AC ISBN 0-399-23010-6
10 9 8 7 6 5 4 3 2 1   First Impression

Come look inside my patch and see
A world of life from A to Z.

The frost is gone, spring is here,
Put the tractor into gear,
Plow the field of weeds and grass—
It's pumpkin-planting time at last!

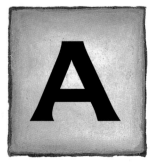

A

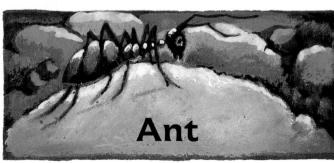

Ant

a

B Beetle **b**

Dig the holes and plant the seeds,

Crow

Keep them watered, pull the weeds.

D

Dragonfly

d

Seeds grow roots, roots take hold,

Earthworm

Stems pop up, leaves unfold.

F

Fly

f

G

Grasshopper

g

Pumpkin vines fill each row,
Leaves are high, blossoms grow.

H

Hummingbird

h

Beneath the blossoms pumpkins form,

Inchworm

Growing fast while it's still warm.

J

Junco

j

Weeds grow faster, day by day,

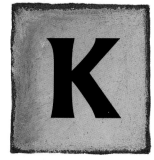

K

Kitten

k

Stop the weeds by spreading hay.

Ladybug

Watch the pumpkins grow till fall,
Orange and ripe, cut them all.

Moth

N

Nuthatch

n

Decorate the pumpkin stand,
Paint a bright new sign by hand.

Owl

Make some scarecrows out of hay—
Pumpkin selling starts today.

P

Pheasant

p

The patch is busy when it's light,

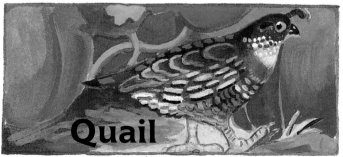

Quail

The patch is busy in the night.

Raccoon

Help your buyers pick and choose
The size and shape just right to use,
Big or small, or in between,
Soon it will be Halloween!

Snail

Toad

T t

Have some pumpkin-carving fun,
Pumpkins grinning when you're done.

U

Underwing Moth

u

Vixen

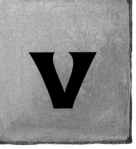

Wren

Let your jack-o'-lanterns greet
Spooky friends who trick-or-treat.

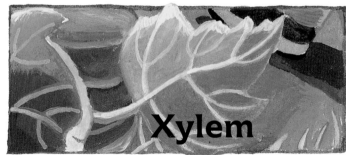

Xylem

FREE
PUMPKINS

Y

Yellow Jacket

y

Now that Halloween is past,
It's time to close the pumpkin patch.

Z

Zebra Butterfly

Z

The weather's changing—time to find
The biggest pumpkin left behind.
Scoop out all the seeds to dry,
Store away your spring supply.

Oil and salt and roast the rest,
Share them with your winter guests.

DISCARDED

PEACHTREE

J 421.1 SLOAT   PTREE
Sloat, Teri
Patty's pumpkin patch

APR 2 4 2000

Atlanta-Fulton Public Library